I0616973

TOBIAS RETURNS

A CALL FOR HELP

TOBIAS BOOK II

BOBBI BOLAND WHITE

WingSpan Press

Copyright 2017 Bobbi Boland White
All rights reserved

This is a work of fiction. Although certain location names are real, and some events may inadvertently resemble actual incidents, all names, dates, places and events in this work are either fictitious or are used fictitiously. No real person living or dead is portrayed in this work.

No part of this book may be reproduced or transmitted in any form or by any means, electronic or mechanical, including photocopying, recording or by any information storage and retrieval system, without written permission from the author, except for the inclusion of brief quotations in reviews.

Published in the United States and the United Kingdom by WingSpan Press, Livermore, CA

The WingSpan name, logo and colophon are the trademarks of WingSpan Publishing.

ISBN 978-1-59594-611-9 (pbk.)

First edition 2017

Printed in the United States of America

Library of Congress Control Number: 2017912440

www.wingspanpress.com

1 2 3 4 5 6 7 8 9 10

*Sometimes it can be
difficult to tell
who is actually an Angel,
and who isn't.*

*It is possible that
even Angels
have this problem.*

A CALL FOR HELP,

Chapter 4

CHAPTER ONE

At 4 a.m. on a moonlit California night, Mira sat straight up in bed, her heart pounding wildly. She listened. The cabin was still. Pushing back the covers, she looked to the window.

The small yard, the surrounding hills, were heavy with silence. Nothing moved –no sound at all. Yet she knew. She had heard it. Her heart had heard it.

Carefully, Mira padded across the floor. She slipped into her jeans and sweatshirt, tossing her nightshirt onto the bed. She found her hiking boots and quickly put them on. She felt in the pocket of her jeans – okay, a few bills, some change. The hallway was dark and the floorboards creaked as she made her way to the closet and pulled down a jacket.

"What are you doing?"

She spun around. It was Ben, her brother, a few years younger but already as tall. "Never mind." She paused. "I have to go somewhere."

"Now?"

Mira nodded. She began walking towards the door but hesitated, turned back. "Ben, do you have any money? Like … about twenty dollars?"

"For what?" Mira didn't answer.

"It's Tobias, isn't it? I felt it too".

Mira took a step toward her brother. "I think he needs help." She paused, "I'm scared, Ben. Maybe he's not dead, after all." She took a breath. "You felt it too?"

Ben nodded. "Wait." He turned back towards his room, "I've got twenty-five." In less than a minute he was back, half-dressed, boots in hand. "I'm coming, Mira." He leaned against the wall, pulling on his boots. "Write a note for Dad. Tell him it's okay – we'll call."

Mira moved into the tiny kitchen, found some paper and began to write: *Dad, we love you. Ben and I are going back to check on Toby's grave. We'll take the Greyhound so it's safe. We'll call you. Love, Mira*

It was a vast, quiet night as they walked side-by-side down the steep hill to the road. The moon was full and shone a pale light on the mountain foothills that stretched and loped behind them. "I'm glad Dad hasn't finished the house in the mountains yet," Ben glanced over at his sister.

Mira didn't answer. "Doesn't matter," she said finally, "we'd still find a way."

"Yeah," Ben sighed. "I can't imagine living up there." He lowered his voice. "Know what I mean?"

Mira nodded. "That's because everything is different now … more empty."

"Yeah," Ben walked with his head down. "Dad hopes we'll forget who's missing. How can we forget?" For a moment he was silent. "And what makes it worse is that even without Mom, at least if we still had Toby …"

Ben stopped, regretting what he had just said, waiting for

the pain in his throat to ease, the picture of Tobias' mangled body.

For a few minutes they walked in silence, lost in their own thoughts of the dog that had found them, changed their lives, and then disappeared.

"There's a truck coming ..." A set of wide headlights was winding down the narrow highway from the village to their north. Mira slowed her pace. "Think they'd give us a ride?"

"They might." Ben was watching the approaching lights. "I'd feel better though, if we had our bikes."

For a brief moment they exchanged looks. Right. Bikes would definitely be better.

They turned back, moving onto the road's shoulder. "I need my cell, anyway, for ... you know ... calling Dad." They were beneath some trees now, in almost complete darkness; the truck sped by without a pause.

"And some I.D." Ben's boots clacked as he moved back onto the road. "Food too," he said, a few paces later. "It's a really long way, Mira."

And it was. If they were lucky it would take almost six hours – two on their bikes and four more on the Greyhound, to reach the closest town to Tobias, to the body of Tobias, to what was left of that body, to the torn and broken, hollowed out remains they only half believed could ever have been their tall and golden beautiful friend, Tobias.

So they prepared, double-checked their provisions, filled their water bottles, locked up the cabin and got their bikes out of the shed.

It was 5:10 a.m. when they reached the edge of town. The

ride from the cabin in the hills, although steep and treacherous, went smoothly and soon the lights of town were visible. Mira smiled as she cruised down the long tree lined streets, the hospital where her mother had worked, the sleeping homes and yards. They were going to do this – yes! There was no going back now.

Forty minutes later they locked their bikes on the library bike rack next to the white science lab that housed their dad's office. "He'll probably check in here first, to write up whatever wildlife he saw overnight." Mira paused. "He'll see our bikes, Ben."

Ben looked toward the mountains. Dawn was approaching; a hint of first light touched the sky; soon it would splash in patches of misty gold through the forested hills. "That's not for awhile yet," he shifted his backpack into a more comfortable position. "Come on; we can text him later. How much time do we have?"

Mira was studying her phone. "Half an hour. The first bus leaves at 6:25. It's about six blocks from here." She flipped her phone closed and looked down the empty street. "Wait." Mira stopped, phone still in hand. Ben, who was a few yards ahead turned back. "Maybe we should take our bikes – keep them with us. We could use them for the final few miles. What do you think?"

"Okay," Ben nodded. "Good idea."

Because the truth was that getting to the little desert outpost on the edge of Death Valley where they had buried Tobias would not be easy. They knew the way – vaguely. They remembered the drive. But now those "last few miles" from the closest town to that outpost which had taken under an hour in their father's truck was looking more like … "It's about 40 miles," Mira was standing under the streetlight staring at her phone, "as the crow flies," she added, because it was actually 52.

But they could handle that later. For now, they needed to get to that little town that was 52 miles away from Toby. Problem was that from all Mira could discover, although this town was on the Interstate, no schedule she could find on her phone included it – nothing seemed to stop there.

But that was okay. They were going to Tobias even if there were no rational way on earth to do it. It was a done deal, a finished fact. Strangely, the flow of time in our universe seems to recognize these kinds of facts – events that haven't happened yet but that somehow jump ahead into the future anyway, and plant themselves so solidly that paths just open up for them.

So after a few more blocks as the sky began to lighten and the first traffic of the day appeared, they reached the Greyhound terminal in San Bernardino and Mira pleaded their case to the ticket agent there.

"What did you tell her?" Ben nudged Mira as the agent came out from her position and motioned for them to follow. Mira didn't answer, intent on staying close behind the agent who was leading them to the outside boarding area where a dozen busses were lined up, their motors rumbling.

The agent Mira and Ben were following moved down the line of busses and approached a driver who had just opened the sliding cargo door on the underside of his bus. He looked up, first at her and then at the children behind her.

"Now what?" Ben glanced over at his sister.

"Hush, Ben." Mira was watching the driver intently, "It's our bikes." She turned over their tickets and began to study the boarding information printed on the ticket envelope. But Ben was one step ahead of her, down on one knee, having already turned and secured her bike's handlebars and working now to immobilize the pedals.

Mira watched in amazement. "How did you learn to do that?"

"Doesn't matter how," Ben was working on his own bike. "Come on," he said, standing, "I bet he'll take us now."

And the driver did.

"So, you think he'll stop for us … even though it's not listed on the schedule?" They were moving down the aisle, settling in, fifth row to their left. Ben studied his sister. "You told that good a lie?"

"Yep, that's what I think. What lie?" Mira tried to use an indignant tone but it didn't work – she was so hugely happy, so greatly relieved that they were pulling out of the station.

"Some group we're supposed to be joining," Ben continued. "You think I didn't hear you? The Desert Adventure Bicycle Tour. Man, Mira, where did you come up with that?"

"On the Internet. Death Valley Tours. It's Spring Break for most schools, not ours yet, but Redlands for example. So it's not a complete lie, not like I'm bearing false witness against someone."

"I'm just saying, Mira. A lie is a lie." He paused, "You need to be careful. People don't trust kids who lie."

Not even if it's for Tobias? Mira frowned, leaning her head against the window. But Ben was probably right. Lying was always a risk. She would definitely stop lying from now on – unless she had to.

So they were on their way. "Ben," Mira was still leaning against the window, watching the sprawl of houses that dotted the landscape as the bus crawled upward towards the mountains and the open desert beyond. "I know it sounds crazy but do you think maybe the dog we buried wasn't really Tobias?"

"It was Tobias." Ben leaned back in his seat, closing his eyes, "It doesn't matter, Mira. That's not the point."

"I just don't understand how this is happening." Mira sighed. "But you're right. It doesn't matter."

After a few moments Ben spoke quietly, "Mira, I think Tobias died a few times, not just once. How did he survive being shot? Just being lucky … that's not enough."

"I know," Mira answered.

"Remember that night by the fire when he suddenly appeared?"

Mira nodded.

"He'd been alone in the desert for a long time – remember? His shoulder was infected; he could hardly walk. But he was perfect. He was … perfect. And then he disappeared again, before we could even touch him."

Mira opened her eyes. She looked over at her brother. "I always thought maybe we just imagined him. That's what Dad said. And nobody wanted to talk about it, all this time. I'm glad you saw him too, Ben."

Ben returned her look. "I absolutely saw him."

Ben looked away. "What I'm trying to say is … even if the parts of him that we found, and buried, were his body, the point is that Tobias, the real Tobias, can get over things like that, can get past them. When it's important enough, maybe he doesn't need his body."

Mira sighed. Her eyes had filled with tears, so she closed them. "Let's not talk about it, Ben," she said quietly.

Because this was Tobias they were talking about – the frightened puppy with the big eyes she had found by the roadside so long ago, the silly playful friend that had won everyone's heart, the long legged golden collie mix who had trusted her completely, who would lay down his life for her, the tall, rangy one year old she had left behind when the family moved, and who had believed her when she told him she'd come back for him.

This was Tobias, the silent presence she had dreamed about and worried about month after month and year after year as the family moved from place to place, only to emerge as if from the dead, a starving half-blind skeleton who had been living in the mines for heaven knows how long or how he even got there, the pads on his paws ripped and bleeding, his shoulder smashed and splintered, collapsing into her arms on a desert road almost four hundred miles from where she had left him.

This was Tobias. And so … he wasn't dead; he couldn't be dead. The remains they had buried could have been any skinny long haired dog whose stomach had been crushed, whose legs were torn loose, and whose head had been blown apart by an overwhelming force. Her father said it was Tobias. Everyone said it was Tobias. But Mira didn't believe it. She pretended to believe it but in her deepest heart, she couldn't.

They had performed the proper ritual however. They had grieved over the poor dog they had found, keeping him with them until they were packed up and leaving the Nevada campsite that had been their home for almost a year.

They buried him in a box with Tobias' blanket, Tobias' favorite rawhide bone, the comb they had used to patiently pull out his burrs, even the old rubber boot he had used as a toy. They said prayers over him, and they dug a resting place for him behind a little chapel on Death Valley's edge with only empty desert and miles of sky to form a cathedral of peace around him.

They did all that for the dog they had found. And it was good to do it. And they were glad they did it. But it wasn't Tobias.

CHAPTER 2

They decided not to call their dad until later. "We need to wait. No point upsetting him;" Mira had explained, "who knows what he might do?"

"Anyway," she added now, settling back in her seat, glancing over at Ben and wondering if he were asleep, "he won't get home until evening, at least," she checked her phone, "so we're safe for awhile."

But *safe* is a relative term, meaning it wasn't Jacob, their father, who would ever startle them, frighten them, pull them out of their seats, interrogate and threaten to arrest them. But someone else would – boarding the bus with another officer, tall and muscular, unannounced, uniformed, gun in the brown holster on his hip, walking fast and hard down the aisle, stopping at their seats, looking down harshly at them and then at the middle aged woman in the aisle seat directly across from them.

"Who are they?" Ben was awake now, whispering to Mira.

"Immigration. Do you have your State I.D. card?"

"Yeah," Ben fumbled in his pocket. "Don't let them see your phone, Mira."

Mira nodded. She felt in her jeans for her drivers permit. Suddenly one of the officers turned to her, indicating the woman across the aisle, "Esta su madre?" Without waiting for an answer, he reached for her arm.

"Hey, take it easy," Ben struggled to get up.

The officer paused. "Watch your mouth, Kid. You and your sister are coming with me." He pulled Mira into the aisle. The other officer was ahead, pushing the woman who had been across from them towards the front of the bus. She was complaining loudly, speaking rapidly in Spanish so that Mira and Ben had no idea what she was saying.

"That's not our mother," Mira was saying. "We don't even know her."

"You don't, eh?" the officer looked down at her with impatience. They had stopped in the aisle; Mira was fumbling for her permit. Meantime Ben had his State I.D. card and reached over with it. The officer squinted. "This is supposed to be you?" He gave Ben a once-over. "Maybe." He handed back the card. "You better hope so, Kid." He took the flimsy copy of Mira's permit, which had been folded and refolded many times, and studied it.

"Our dad's from Israel," Mira began bravely, "He's a scientist. My brother looks like him but I don't." ...*Oh no,* Ben was thinking, *because it never was good when Mira began rambling* ... " I look like my mom." Mira took a breath.

The officer shook his head, "Never mind who you look like." They had begun moving again, "You're breaking the law and you know it. The two of you are underage, so if that's not your mother," he indicated the Spanish woman being led off the bus by the other officer, "then you're traveling alone." He looked down at Mira. "Even worse – right?"

The officer, still holding Mira, started down the steps motioning Ben to go in front of them. The door was open and the woman being interrogated by the first officer was standing outside. The driver quieted the motor to an idle.

In a moment they were off the bus. The driver was waiting however, watching. The first immigration officer now turned to Mira. He was looking carefully at her permit. "How old are you?"

"Fifteen."

"Un huh. What school do you go to?"

"Redlands. I'm in tenth. We're meeting up with a tour group from our school – for Spring Break."

The first officer scrutinized Ben, checking him out from head to toe. He returned Ben's I.D. card, and began with the questions. "What's your favorite team?"

"Lakers," Ben answered.

"Player?"

"Kobe"

"Got a dog?"

Ben nodded.

"What kind – what breed?"

"Golden mix – got some collie in him."

"Your father know you're here?"

"Yes Sir."

"Is he at work now?"

Ben nodded.

"Give me the phone number."

"There is no phone. He's in the mountains on a project.

He works for the Conservancy. Do you want our home phone?"

"Is your mother home?"

"No, Sir. We haven't seen our mother in more than two years."

The officer moved away. He opened his phone.

"Why did you say all that about dad?" Ben moved closer to his sister. The second officer had released her.

"I don't know. I thought it made us sound ... more acceptable. Why does it matter?"

Ben didn't answer. He was trying to lip-read what the first officer was saying into his phone. He turned back to Mira. "It sounds like he's checking for runaways that fit our description."

They waited.

Ben sighed. He looked up at the driver who was watching the whole scene through the open door. The driver glanced past him to the two officers, shaking his head just slightly. He leaned forward, hunched over the steering wheel with a bored expression as if he had been through this before

"I think we're okay," Ben looked back at his sister. "I think they're just doing their job, checking for people who shouldn't be here, ... or, whatever."

"Maybe." Mira was shivering. Her jacket had been left on the bus and the morning air was cold.

"California State I.D. is California State I.D," Ben said, his courage building. "Can't argue with that."

He was right. Even their 'madre' must have checked out, because after five more minutes standing on the side of the road, all three were permitted to re-board the bus.

"Wonder what she told them," Ben said to Mira as they slid back into their seats.

"Hi, Mom," he waved to their neighbor, leaning forward as the bus pulled out.

"Ben, you are so crazy," Mira elbowed him back into his seat. But of course she was smiling too.

CHAPTER 3

It was 10:20 a.m., fifty-five minutes past the single scheduled stop on Mira's ticket, when the bus swung from the highway, traveled for a short distance along an access road and came to a sudden stop next to a small Travel Plaza. The doors opened.

"Five minute cigarette break; get your coffee and make it speedy," the driver announced. "This is an express, no more stops."

"This is it," Mira stood up. "Remember? Dad stopped here for gas."

The driver was signaling to Ben and Mira, moving down the steps in front of them.

In less than six minutes they had their bikes and the bus was moving back onto the highway. They stood watching it disappear. Wow – they were here. Only 40 more miles (as the crow flies.)

So they were off – bikes untied, backpacks on, deep blue sky above.

They were completely alone, moving in silence through the first mile of scattered homes, a humble church, a few small ranches, lost in thought as the desert opened up before them, stretching out on either side, stretching long and low behind them.

It was amazingly empty – no signs of human life at all. But it was cool, and the desert sunlight was pale and playful, moving along low hills and dunes, touching upon the scarlet buds of cacti flowers waking into spring.

It was the kind of desert morning that settles slowly on a person, like a prayer, an instinctive bowing of the spirit to the majesty of creation. A person feels small, as if he is moving through sky, through time, as if he is the only person on earth – the first person.

Animals feel it too, a certain stillness of the spirit, an awe that was real long before words were real, and which is still more real than words could ever be.

For Ben and Mira, however, the feeling encompassed more than awe.

This was the Mojave. The Mojave that had been Tobias' home. The Mojave that had taken his body. The Mojave from which he had called them. So mile after mile they rode without speaking, with only their thoughts, no one on the road before them, no one on the road behind.

They were eight miles into the open desert when they saw the first sign: Shoshone 40 miles. Yes, that's it! Five more miles and they were able to take a brief break, pulling off the road onto a small paved area with a faint trail rolling into the desert and a rare bushy tree to (thankfully) pee behind.

When they reached the halfway point they were exhausted. The two-lane road rolled slightly. It had no real shoulders, just narrow half-shoulders of loose sand and gravel. At first, there had been low hills in the distance but soon multi-colored mountains rose before them.

They had passed a call box in the first hour, smiling to themselves at how "old fashioned" this road must be, but when the second call box appeared they began to reconsider. Mira took out her cell and tried to call home. "No service," she called over her shoulder to Ben. Her brother nodded. Now they knew why there were call boxes, although they were for emergency services only, certainly not to call their Dad.

In Mira's opinion, halfway or not, they shouldn't rest yet. Ahead lay a long climb; once they had braved it, she told Ben, then they could rest.

But it was a wicked, strength sapping climb … up and up for almost two miles then down slightly, curving so that they could not see what lay ahead as the road rolled and dipped in gradual descent, then leveled briefly before it climbed again.

DUMONT DUNES: a simple sign on a post by the road and a disappearing trail that seemed to lead to nowhere.

They stopped by the sign. For a few minutes they rested – just to breathe, to take a gulp or two of water from their thermoses, to look around before continuing. The mountains to their east had receded and were barely visible. Only a low line of hills rose from the desert floor. But that was it. There was nothing else to look at.

They couldn't know. How could they know of the existence of a sandy road that emerged from behind those distant dunes, continuing for several miles along a wide, shallow, winding river filled with an array of white rocks, a mystical place where migrating birds could stop to drink. Sperry Wash: a resting place for many animals, large and small.

They would miss it. They would continue on the narrow two lane paved road from which they could see nothing of the life-giving oasis beyond the trail to Dumont Dunes.

Others had paused there also, looked out but then continued on, discouraged by the seeming emptiness. But perhaps it was all for the best. Perhaps the animals and birds were safer that way.

Pedaling hard now, Dumont Dunes fading behind them, the road beginning to rise again.

An hour later, still climbing. Another call box.

"How much longer?" Ben wiped his face. He checked the sun. They had reached the top of the highest hill and were looking down upon a vast desert valley. The day was lengthening, approaching mid afternoon.

"Not much; maybe a few hours." Mira took a gulp of water, letting a few drops dribble onto her hand and wetting her forehead with them. "We were covering almost eight miles an hour but lately," she paused for breath, "when we were climbing, it really slowed us down."

"Did you try texting Dad?"

Mira nodded. "It said: error, service restrictions, no text sent." She took a breath. "It's still okay," she said after another breath, meaning they possibly had a few more hours before he arrived home from work and got their note.

"Anyway," she turned and looked at her brother, "what can we do?"

The last thing Ben wanted to do was laugh at his sister. But she was a sight to see all right, standing on the top of this empty hill, straddling her bike, her face and hair soaked with sweat, lines of dirt streaming down from the smudges made by her helmet which hung now against her back, long ago removed in hopes of the slightest breeze to cool her scalp.

Her long dark hair that had been gathered up was now askew; damp tendrils stuck to her face, trailing along the sides of her neck. All this and she looked so serious. So fierce. So grim and determined. No, Ben sure didn't want to laugh. But it took work, some serious work, not to.

"Let's go, then." Ben smiled. He turned away, anticipating the long downward ride before them. "We need to make it before dark. They must have cell service in Shoshone. Right?"

Well, not quite. But we'll get to that.

They were actually doing very well, and the two mile long downward ride from the 2,000 foot hilltop to the desert floor was wildly exhilarating – hair flying, legs outstretched. "Ride the white line," Mira called because there was actually a narrow, paved shoulder here with a ten inch white line to separate it from the road. So down and down they went, riding the white line.

It was almost 4 p.m. They had traveled 42 miles in under 6 hours, and in 40 more minutes they reached a turn off labeled Old Spanish Trail.

They stopped. A small sign read: Village of Tacopa. For a moment they studied it.

It was tempting. Although their surroundings were as desolate as ever, the road to Tacopa was nicely paved, veering east for awhile, then northeast before it disappeared between the hills.

"Maybe this is where Tobias is, in Tacopa, not Shoshone."

Ben was sitting on the side of road, his bike beside him. "Didn't Dad turn off somewhere?"

"I'm not sure," Mira sat down beside him. "Maybe." She sighed, "I didn't even see this place on the map."

"Let's try it," Ben looked over at his sister. "It can't be far and it's in our same general direction.

"There must be water there," he continued, squinting at disappearing road.

Mira didn't answer. "No," she said finally, getting up. "We only have about ten more miles to Shoshone."

"Isn't it more like fifteen?"

"No – well maybe. But for all we know, Tacopa is a ghost town." Mira stood up, straightening her bike. "Remember how many ghost towns we found in Nevada?"

Ben sighed. Mira looked down at him, "Ben?"

But Ben was exhausted. He wasn't moving. "It can't hurt to look," he said. "I need water really bad, Mira."

So Tacopa it was.

At first they regretted the decision. A mile of salt flats on either side, on and on. However when two vehicles, both trucks, soon rumbled by on their way to Tacopa, their hopes revived. At least there would be humans there, maybe even a few houses.

When some low hills appeared, things started looking even better. One more hill, some welcome tree shade over the road and the picturesque town of Tacopa materialized.

The first building they saw was a chapel.

It was a lonely white chapel, its steeple outlined against the red sky of the descending sun. There it was – the chapel where six months ago they had left Tobias. Or was it?

Sometimes, especially when a person (or an animal for that matter) is exhausted or confused by a series of events he hasn't had time to synthesize, to put into the proper order, it's easy to hallucinate.

Even later, upon remembering a scene – how it looked, how the light was on it, it can be difficult to know if it were real, or just a dream. That's how this chapel looked: the almost real but not-quite-real way things look in a dream.

So they stared. Could this really be it?

"You think maybe ..."

"I don't know. Sure looks like it, same steeple and everything."

"But, it's not," Mira eyes began to sting. Her voice wavered but the tears, just below the surface, stayed there. "There are houses up the hill behind it. See them? Our chapel was isolated – all alone, remember?"

"Yeah," Ben continued staring. He saw the houses but he wasn't sure. "I guess you're right," he said finally. "It's weird, though.

"Let's look for a store," Ben remounted his bike, "Come on," he turned to his sister. "You get too emotional, Mira. Don't worry. We'll find Tobias." And he started up the road.

CHAPTER 4

Tacopa turned out to be friendly. They passed a closed post office, a few homes, and then a small store appeared. The door was open, the lights were on, and the local water was sweet and free.

For hot food, they were advised, a 24 hour coffee shop was only three miles north of where they stood. And, they were told with a smile, another four miles and they would be back on the road to Shoshone.

In summary, the total distance to Shoshone was less than 12 miles – an easy ride, yes?

This information, although helpful, was processed slowly. "Um … okay, thanks but," Mira was so hot and tired she felt dizzy, "is there cell service here?"

"No, sorry," came the answer. And the land phone at the little store was for local calls only.

It was getting dark. What to do? They had no idea. So they sat on a bench outside the store and let exhaustion sink into their bones, and into their limbs, and into their brains. This actually felt good – so good that Ben fell asleep sitting up.

The next scene, that looked like it might be a dream, appeared just as darkness settled softly on their heads, the bench, the little store.

They very well could have been angels – an old man, a young man, and a girl. But it's a good bet they were humans after all, just campers stopping for supplies. They came on horses, clopping quietly up to the store, not bothering to tie the reins, looping them and letting them fall in confidence their equine friends would wait for them, which they did.

It was all so easy, so relaxed, that when the possibly-angels-but-probably-campers returned a few minutes later, it seemed natural and comfortable to say hello.

"Hi," the young girl said, standing in front of Mira. "You guys need a campsite for the night? We're right down the road."

And then the young man approached, leading his horse, a sorrel mare that looked almost as tired as Mira. "You could follow us," he said smiling, "or," and he indicated an empty saddle pad, secured over thick sheepskin, "you could hitch a ride on Molly, here."

Yep, miracles like this can actually happen. Normally, of course, it's not so easy. Angels don't just "appear" when you need them. And angels on horseback are very rare.

So that's how Mira and Ben ended up sleeping in the glow of a lone campfire, under a sky full of stars, listening to the songs and prayers of the desert, the yips of coyotes and the hooting of owls. They were, of course, ravenously hungry so that the plates of beans and crusty bread offered to them seemed like a feast indeed.

They were sitting on a fallen tree trunk as they ate,

watching the faces and smiles of their possibly-angel-proba-bly-camper benefactors. And just like those of their benefactors, their own faces were flushed from the heat of the fire and their own eyes glowed golden in the shifting shadows of the night.

Sometimes it is difficult to tell just who is actually an angel and who isn't. It's possible that even angels have this problem.

Mira and Ben didn't say much, only that they were looking for their dog – a collie mix, basically bronze with some darker markings, but a beautiful reddish gold in the light. They didn't explain that he was dead – supposedly dead. That's not the kind of thing you say to an angel, or even a possible-angel.

And yet, amazingly, in this dream that wasn't a dream, the young man who wasn't an angel, mentioned that a dog matching the description of Tobias had been seen several times in those hills. "Do you have a picture of him?" he asked Mira.

"Ah, yes … very similar," he said as he held a small photo from Ben's wallet up to the light, "…very similar." But the photo was an old one, taken when Toby was young, before they had lost him, before he had changed.

Mira remembered Ben's photo. It showed a Tobias she hardly remembered. In the photo there was no record of the pain he had suffered – his large eyes sunken into hollows and the bones of his forehead sharp and visible.

"He's different now," she explained. "He's much older." The young man nodded, handing the photo back to Ben. "He may have a limp," she added softly. "We just don't know how he may look."

It was at that point that the old man spoke. His voice was low and rumbly and because he sat back from the fire it was difficult to hear. "The dog seen here was very young," he said to Mira, "too young to be your dog. He's with others like himself, and a very wise female is looking after him. In the morning you must go on with your journey.

"But," he added after a moment of silence, "just to set your minds at ease, this younger dog is safe. He is where he should be."

And that was that. So with those words Mira and Ben settled down to sleep.

They lay in a small clearing beside the north end of a narrow six mile trail that twisted down through the dark hills, meandering between tall trees and growing brush, winding through the black walls of shadowed canyons and then magically opening up and spreading into the wide shallows of a hidden watering place where the moonlight played upon thousands of smooth white rocks. Sperry Wash.

But even here, in the impeccable silence of the desert night, Mira and Ben could hear its source.

"It's the Amargosa," Mira whispered, lifting up on one elbow. "It has to be," she looked at Ben who was also awake and equally awestruck, "all the way from Nevada, all the way from our campsite in Nevada."

And it was. They lay close to it – to where it moved slowly, deep in the undergrowth. This was the rough beginning of the Amargosa River Trail; it was here that the saving waters of the Amargosa emerged, bringing life to the desert, to the small towns and campsites, giving hope to the bobcats and cougars, to coyotes and elk, to sheep and to deer.

"Toby would find it." Ben looked at his sister, "if he were anywhere close to the Amargosa, Toby would find it.

"Maybe the old man was wrong," he whispered to Mira, just before he fell asleep. "Or maybe he lied. Mira, Toby could be close, right here, watching over us the way he always did."

It was almost midnight when Ben opened his eyes. He looked over at his sister who was sitting up in the moonlight, her phone open.

"Are you texting Dad?"

"Trying to. Nevada should be over there," she indicated the eastern hills beyond Tacopa, "and you never know..." Because several times in the mountains at home when "no service" was the response to an attempted call, a text would suddenly go through.

"Right." Ben watched her, "What does it say?"

"Sent." Mira closed her phone. "But ... we'll have to see," she said quietly, meaning *sent* doesn't necessarily mean *received*.

CHAPTER 5

Mira's text was brief: *Dad, all is good. Safe in Tacopa. Shoshone tomorrow. C U soon? xoxo.*

It's not easy to describe the huge relief that Jacob felt upon receiving that text. He was still awake in the cabin just above the valley of San Bernardino. For hours he had been waiting for the children's call, pacing, studying his maps, looking up bus schedules and routes, searching for possible stopping points along the final lonely road to Shoshone.

Okay. Whew. He closed his phone and secured it in the duffle bag he had hastily packed. He could rest now – they were safe. He would leave before dawn, take the mountain trail, then cross the high desert on a narrow unpaved road that would save an hour on his journey to meet them. Jacob took out an orange and threw it into the bag. He would need to check the truck, get gas, but that could wait.

Jacob turned off the light. *Thank You, Lord,* he prayed as he walked into his room and collapsed on the bed. His eyes closed.

He never heard the rain begin – so fine, so light that it

made no sound as it veiled the hills with mist, the scattered homes, the disappearing streetlights below.

He never heard the first few serious drops, the ping ping on the roof of his truck, the gentle movements of the leaves in the tree outside his window.

He may have been aware, just slightly as he slept, of the slow and steady drumming of the rain around his dreams, but it was almost dawn and his sleep was deep when the sky opened fully, pouring walls of water down from the sky, pounding the ground without mercy, flooding the trails, the mountain roads, making the shortcuts he had planned invisible, washed out, impassable.

The storm had come without warning, out of the Pacific, up from Baja, making a sudden unexpected turn from its projected path, crossing the mountains, angling inland and then, like a dog on a scent, lowering its head and following the San Andreas northward, filling ravines and river beds, rushing over streets and roads.

Jacob stood at the door of his home. It was 5:30 a.m. and the forecast wasn't good. Estimated as six miles wide, the storm was spreading north and eastward towards Nevada, stranding interstate truckers in heavy fog, forcing cars and SUVs onto off-ramps where frightened drivers fumbled for cell phones, watching in horror as the water rose.

Jacob was patient. He knew that the local flooding would soon subside; the fog over the hills and the interstate would lift and traffic would resume its uphill creep.

But he also knew that danger still loomed. The storm was waiting, playing hide and seek over the mountains, hovering over the high desert that he must cross. Jacob prepared his supplies. Soon the low clouds that were traveling north would thicken, turn purple then black, preparing to unleash their fury once again. The storm would re-emerge, its strength intact.

Jacob locked up the cabin. Time to go. There was no way he could outrun the storm but he could try to get a jump on it.

The small town from which his children had called him, as well as the even smaller one to which they were headed, would not be spared. The desert floor was hard, could not absorb the heavy rains. Flash flooding would fill the land rushing along with deadly force. Fences would weaken; structures would loosen and be washed away. And then it struck him – the grave.

CHAPTER 6

Ben and Mira were up and on the way to Shoshone before dawn. The campsite had been swept clean, the angels gone. All that remained was a loosely woven red shawl that someone had placed over Mira while she slept. The shawl had been knitted by hand, large loops of yarn displaying the signs and symbols of America's First Shoshone Nation, the Native Americans for whom the land where they had left Tobias was named.

"I wonder what it means, Ben – the language on the shawl." Mira was riding parallel to her brother on the open road, the shawl in her backpack. It was cool and the sky of first-light was streaked with long wisps of ashen grey so that she hardly noticed that the sky was quickly darkening behind her, filling with clouds that were menacing and heavy – the color of lead where they lay low over the mountains to her west.

Ben dismissed Mira's comment. He glanced at his sister, then up at the sky, "It's going to rain. Come on." He leaned forward, moving ahead and looking back over his shoulder, "Let's go. Can't you smell it?"

Ben wasn't being rude. If he had nothing to say about a

subject, he said nothing. That's just how he was. "Okay?" he continued, smiling because he knew that Mira understood. They had to go; the shawl could wait.

The approach to Shoshone was gentle. Rounding a bend with mounds of sandy earth on either side, the land opened and the first structure appeared in the distance outlined against the grey sky, its white steeple unmistakable.

Their hearts were beating double-time as they approached.

The chapel stood on a low hill, back from the road. There was nothing around it - no other buildings, nothing but desert and sky. They dismounted their bikes walking them up the gravel drive and then along the narrow path that circled behind the church.

At the end of the path they stopped.

"There she is," Ben whispered. "She's right where we buried him."

Mira looked in amazement at her brother. She also saw the thin form of a lone coyote laying on a rise of land next to the flat, half buried stone they had placed over Tobias. What did he mean, "she?"

They stood transfixed, straddling their bikes, breathing as quietly as possible. Because although the coyote was still a good 40 yards away, she had seen them; she was watching them, ears up, her golden eyes and soft buff-color coat adapted perfectly to the faint light of the desert dawn.

She's beautiful, Mira was thinking. *Why is she laying by Toby's grave? Does she think that he's in there?*

"Ben...?" Mira turned to her brother, "how did you know...?" But it was over. The desert was empty. The coyote was gone.

They walked their bikes across the dry land, pushing onto the spot where six months ago they had buried Tobias. They stopped. The slightly irregular slab of granite, 10"x16", which marked his grave had sunken slightly into the ground.

The inscription, which had been carefully planned, cut out and placed tightly over the stone so that the ancient sandblaster Jacob had borrowed could do its work, was still there. It wasn't perfect but it was there:

TOBIAS
SAFE WITH GOD

REMEMBER US

Mira knelt by the stone. She brushed if off. *Oh, Toby,* she thought, *what can we do? Why did you call us?* She looked up. *It's so lonely here.*

But then she saw, next to the stone, right beside her, hoof prints! Two horses had been there; no, *three* horses had been there!

"Ben, look!"

"I know. I see them; they headed north." Ben moved several yards away, following the prints. "I'm not sure but I think Toby's friend went north too." He bent down close to the ground. "Her prints are so light, so small." Mira left her bike and moved up beside him, "I see them too, but … "

"Yeah, I know." Ben looked at her, "They're gone, end right here." He sighed. "Let's search around and see if we can pick them up again."

For the next twenty minutes they searched in vain. The

rain had begun – a soft, fine rain. Ben straightened, looking into the distance. "Want to follow the horse prints while we still can?"

Mira didn't answer. "Why?" she said finally.

Ben studied the range of hills to their north. He turned back to Mira, "Because maybe they're all together. Maybe she's with them."

"So? I don't think we should, Ben. Badwater is that way. It's Death Valley. What would be the point?"

Mira felt the rain and lifted her face to it. "We should go into town," she paused, "dry off and eat something." She studied her brother, "Aren't you hungry?"

But Ben wasn't moving. Mira sighed, "What if Dad got my text?" she tried again. "He could be on the way, right now. With the truck," she said finally, clinching the deal.

So they retrieved their bikes, walked back to the road, and pedaled into the tiny town of Shoshone. It's a good thing they did because in the ten minutes it took to arrive at Shoshone's only coffee shop that stood like a warm beacon on the empty road, the sky had darkened and rumbled above them. Ben doubled down on his bike, his back bent, and Mira followed his lead.

By the door to the coffee shop, next to a short fence, they stopped. No one spoke as the rain increased and they worked to remove the locks and chains beneath the seats of their bikes, preparing to loop them around the fence's single rail. Ben glanced over at his sister, began to speak but paused. Something had been left unsaid.

"I saw her once before, in Nevada."

Mira looked up.

"She came for him, Mira, that night by the fire. I saw her. I saw her eyes. She was waiting for him."

Mira stood motionless, her lock in her hand, "You never said."

"I know. I'm sorry. But I saw her. I'm sure. She came for him and so … he went with her."

"I always wondered," Mira closed the lock. She was soaked with rain – her hair, her face, "why he never came back."

Ben straightened. He looked directly at his sister, "He was better off with her," he said. "Maybe she was sent to take care of him."

"Whatever," Mira turned away. Because it was true that at the time Toby was still the subject of widespread concern, still a prize to whoever could catch him. Approaching their campsite that one last time could have cost him his freedom, if not his life.

Mira put her hand on the coffee shop door. She couldn't look at her brother right now. She was trying to be glad for Toby, trying not to feel betrayed. Of course he was better off in the wild, better off with *her* in the wild. So why did it hurt? Why did it hurt like this?

Mira opened the door. She knew exactly how she looked, disheveled and dripping in the doorway, a puddle of rainwater at her feet. But just as if it didn't matter, the few faces that turned to her nodded and smiled, and with the welcoming aroma of hotcakes and syrup drifting her way, Mira blushed. *I should be happy for Toby,* she was thinking. *I should be grateful for his friend!*

"You know what I'm thinking?" she said to Ben, jacket pulled off, getting comfortable in the small booth, "I'm thinking she'll help us find him. I'm thinking she knows where he is."

The rain would force Jacob to stop in Daggett. By 9 a.m., four inches of water had covered the narrow desert road he had chosen.

To avoid the storm, he had traveled southwest from the cabin, climbing the base of the mountain from a safer angle, then turning north and swinging wide of the hilltop lakes to make a steep descent with the hills a protecting wall as the storm raged on behind them.

It would catch him soon, he realized, picking up speed as he reached level ground, straightening out and continuing along a sparsely traveled route into the high desert.

But when it did catch him, when the wide beginnings of it first moved over him, it was even worse than he feared.

The rain was fierce, sheeting the windows of his truck like mirrors. The water on the road was rolling along in a river of loose sand and gravel obscuring the cracks of broken concrete beneath it, spreading out over the flat land on either side so that without the occasional utility pole running parallel, it would be impossible to know if the road was still there.

Jacob slowed. He wiped his forehead and checked the dashboard clock. He had come halfway in almost zero traffic. Time to detour, head out to the interstate.

Jacob stopped for coffee at 9:00 a.m. He had forgotten to fill up with gas before he left and was relieved to see a lone service station at the approach to the Interstate. Opening his phone he typed: *On the way.*

He waited.

Sent.

CHAPTER 7

"Lets go sit at the counter," Mira said suddenly. They were still in the booth, counting their change. "We can ask about Toby."

"We're looking for our dog," she explained, trying the waitress first. "Do you live around here? Have you seen an old dog? He's a collie mix, part golden retriever."

The room had stilled – not a sound. Mira turned. The few locals having coffee at the end of the counter were looking at her with interest. The cook, a large friendly looking man, came out from the kitchen, wiping his hands on a rag; he stopped, a slight scowl on his face.

"He has an old injury," Mira was looking at the cook now, trying to read that scowl. "We last saw him over by the chapel on the edge of town."

For several more moments the room was silent. Then, one of the men at the end of the counter spoke up, "Only thing around here is coyotes. Got one crazy female on suicide watch up there at that church – been comin every night for months, stays until dawn." He paused. "Has a pup with her sometimes."

"We saw her today." Mira looked at the man who had spoken, "She was alone."

"Probably got her pup hid." The man took a drink of his coffee. "There's ranchers plan to kill them pups of hers – figure they're gettin too big, bound to be trouble."

He paused. "They'll kill her too, soon as they can locate her pups. She's smarter than they are, though – got those pups hid good, all but that one she keeps with her."

"How many?" Mira leaned forward, almost standing. All eyes were on her but she hardly noticed. "How many pups does she have?"

"Don't know," the man she had addressed turned to his neighbor, "What'd you say, Willie?"

Willie, the man sitting next to him, answered, "Four, maybe five. One of 'em wandered right into town a few times – 'member that, Ella?"

The waitress nodded.

"Friendly little critter," Willie was smiling to himself as he talked. "No fear – no fear at all. Big Mike fired off a few loud ones at him …bam …bam… kicked up some dust to scare him off." He paused, looking back at Mira. "Might save his life some day."

Willie continued looking at Mira, his voice suddenly serious. "Coyotes considered varmints – that's their legal definition, open season on 'em all year long. No better than rats, according to some folks. Worse." Willie smiled the kind of fake smile that means the opposite. "Rats ain't near as bad – right, Ella? At least rats don't steal your chickens."

"Ain't true, Willie, and you know it," the waitress spoke up. "There's no coyotes stealing chickens round here. And that little one begs nice and polite, sits up and wags his tail just like a dog.

"Those cowboys from over the mountain enjoy what they're doin," she continued, "get drunk and think it's fun. Ain't a reason in the world to go out huntin coyotes."

"I know. I know." But Willie wasn't finished messing with Ella. "That female got a nice fur coat on her;" Willie paused, "that's a reason, ain't it?"

"If it's legal to kill coyotes," Mira spoke up, "couldn't someone just as easily kill a dog? I mean would they really do that? Could they get away with that?"

"Thing is," Willie's voice gentled. "Thing is … nobody's watching what these cowboys do. There's no huntin allowed, varmints included, not even with traps, poison – you name it, up the road in Death Valley. But nobody's up there. Don't you see? When nobody's watching, people do what they want."

Again the room was silent.

Mira looked around. The cook had disappeared back into the kitchen. *He knows something,* Mira was thinking. *They all do. It's like they have bad news, but they don't want to say what it is.*

"The coyote you saw in town," Ben reached for his wallet, "did he look like this?" Ben held up the small damp photo of a young Toby.

When no one answered or moved to look at the picture, the waitress who was standing close by, leaned in, took the photo and held it up to the light. "No … well, maybe a little."

Willie stood up. "All right. That's enough. Let me see the photo, Ella."

The waitress moved down the counter. For a long minute

Willie studied the photo. Slowly he shook his head, handing back the photo and sitting down again.

Ella returned the photo to Ben and sighed, "Sorry, Honey." She began wiping the counter. "You'd be best to get a new dog. An orphan pup maybe – that'd be nice."

Ella was still looking down at her work, cleaning and cleaning the same spot. "All the same, you might find yours." She looked up for a moment at the children's faces. "And don't you concern yourself about that little coyote family neither. They'll be fine. They'll survive just fine."

Ella turned away. She had no idea why she felt so sad. A wave of grief had washed right over her – not worry exactly, not concern for the children's safety, just sorrow, the kind of sorrow that encompasses everything, all the world, all the hidden unnamed ways that suffering can trap and hurt the innocent, the young.

Nobody noticed this reaction of Ella's, except perhaps the cook who came out of the kitchen and stood watching as the children laid their dollars on the counter, put on their jackets and headed for the door. He waited until the door had closed behind them.

When he spoke his voice was strong. Everyone looked up.

"I don't know what kind of game those kids are playing on you, Ella, but that dog they say they're looking for is dead. They'll never find him cuz they buried him. I saw it. Came in a truck about six months ago. You saw them too, Willie. We both went out to see what they done."

"I remember," Willie looked up. "Creepy, ain't it?" He shook his head. "Life stinks for kids sometimes, makes 'em act stupid – tryin to cancel out what's done and finished. The dead is dead. They don't come back."

"How do you know it's the same dog – the one they're looking for?" someone asked.

"Name on the stone," Willie said simply. "Same as the name on that little picture."

"Tobias," the cook said. "Hard name to forget. Tobias."

What Willie didn't realize was that Ben hadn't closed the door completely. He was standing outside, pulling up the hood on his jacket when he heard Willie's comment: *The dead is dead – they don't come back.*

"How does he know that?" Ben said to his sister, as they prepared to mount their bikes for the short trip to the town's only motel. "That's what I don't get about people. They act like they know it all. But they don't. Maybe the dead do come back, maybe in a different form, as spirits or angels. Suppose a person or an animal found himself in another universe or dimension, and suddenly he remembered something and he felt that he needed to go back. Who can say God doesn't allow this?"

Mira looked at her brother. "You're right," she said finally. But she was thinking of other things. Where was their Dad?

CHAPTER 8

T hey leaned their bikes against the wall, under a narrow overhang, beside the motel door marked Office. The door was locked. Ben moved down the row of doors trying each one carefully. "Here's an open one," he called softly to Mira.

So that's where they were an hour later, dry and warm, crossing the room barefoot to open the door, socks laid out over the heating unit under the window, when the manager appeared.

Not all kids know this but motel rooms left unlocked when the office is closed are usually saying, "make yourself at home; you can pay later."

The message this gives is that most strangers can be trusted. True enough. On the practical side, it's highly un-likely that a moving van from L.A. is going to pull up to a 1 or 2 star motel on a desert road and start taking out their 10 year old beds and TV sets. Not to say this couldn't happen. But odds are slim.

Moments before the manager arrived, Mira had been looking at a letter-size paper with the motel information on it. "The manager is Theodore Gabrinski," she read to Ben. "Too bad we don't have cash. We could put our money in his mailbox and not have to answer any questions."

Because, oh yes, there would be questions. It was someone from the café who had gone to wake Mr. Gabrinski from his morning nap and tell him about the kids who claimed to be looking for their dead dog. Ella had advised waiting. Their father was probably close by, she had insisted; why not wait until he shows up?

But an hour later there was still no car, no truck, not even another bike at the motel. Just those two lonely bicycles propped up on either side of door #3.

"Our dad is on the way. Meantime, I can pay you with this." Mira, who had just received the text from her father, held out a prepaid Visa card she had received last Christmas. They had left the room and followed the manager to his office.

The manager sat down stiffly at his desk and turned on his computer. He studied the children. Runaways probably. Sheriff wouldn't be by till late tomorrow, came in for the five o'clock mass down at the chapel. But as long as the information about these kids was out there – and he would make sure that it was, any missing teen reports or any other relevant sightings of these two, could be linked to the profile he was setting up.

Missing kids – there were hundreds of them. But this was 2012. Just because a town was considered minimally developed didn't mean they didn't have the power of the Internet at their disposal.

"Where did you get the card?"

"It's mine." Mira was holding her phone. "Here, you can

text my Dad yourself. Or you can call him but you may not get through because he's on the road somewhere and there could be lots of flooding."

The manager lit a cigarette. He was thin, grey hair, rumpled shirt. His teeth were crooked and slightly yellowed but his voice and his eyes were kind so that the children relaxed. Just be polite, Mira had cautioned Ben on the way over from Room 3.

"What are your names? You're from where? Let me see some I.D." There was nowhere to sit in the motel office so in the thirty minute grilling that followed, Mira and Ben stood quietly, answering questions as best they could.

Most of the time, however, the manager wasn't listening, just making notes about their appearance and their attitudes which he had to admit seemed decent enough. He made copies of their I.Ds. on a printer that took a good ten minutes to warm up and asked them if they were hungry. There was a general store behind the service station up the road if they needed anything.

The whole interrogation seemed strange because it swung between overly intimidating to, on the other hand, overly accommodating. Actually, the manager was just trying to wake up. For all he knew someone important could be looking for these kids. His motel, he himself, could end up on the news in no time flat.

Finally, the manager ran out of questions. Now what? He wasn't going to try to contact their "dad." The sheriff could handle that part of it. By the way, he was thinking, what kind of dad would let his kids go off alone, on bikes, 50 miles into nowhere? As long as he kept them here, safe and dry in one of his rooms, Theodore Gabrinski, motel manager and retired postmaster of the historic village of Shoshone, had done his part. So he let them go.

It was mid afternoon when they regrouped, sitting on one of the two double beds in room #3 as the rain drummed on outside. They had walked around town, visited the store and the adjoining museum. They had asked about Tobias. They had asked if anyone had seen three campers on horses. But all they got were empty looks. No one, it seemed, had seen anything.

The museum, however, had a small section of books and Mira found one on "The animals of the Mojave." The photo of a golden-eyed coyote resting by the opening to a partially camouflaged den sent shivers down Mira's spine. *I'm really stupid,* she was thinking. *Of course the pups are Toby's. Maybe their mother is staying close to the grave so he can find her when he comes back.* But she had to stop there because she knew it made no sense. How could he be in the grave and still come back?

Well, suppose he wasn't in the grave; suppose the mother simply recognized his scent was there. Coyote's have an even better sense of smell than dogs, she was reading, bending down and peering at the pages in the dull light of the museum.

"Hey look, Mira," Ben had found a dusty display towards the back of the room. "Giraffe bones!" he called, "there were once giraffes out here! In the desert!" He approached her. "What would they eat?" he asked, noticing the book in her hand but ignoring it. "Don't they eat leaves from the tops of trees? What trees?

"What's the matter?" Ben realized it was hopeless. He bent slightly and read the title on the book in Mira's hands. "Let's go," he looked up at her. "You can ask the woman in front if you can borrow it – ok?" Maybe it will explain about the Giraffe bones, he was thinking.

If it did, Ben would never find out. But at least it was full of information about coyotes.

"Nine months," Mira told him, once they were back in their room. "Pups stay with their mom until they are nine months. Just think, the whole time Toby was being hunted as some kind of killer, she was having his pups. And when he disappeared and we couldn't find him, he was with her. It says, coyotes are very loyal to their mates. Male coyotes even help the females raise their pups. They guard the den. Oh, Ben, maybe Toby was helping with his pups."

"He's not a coyote, Mira," Ben sighed. He was never going to get a chance with that book. "But I know what you mean; he would have helped her if he could."

It was getting late. Mira opened the motel room door and looked out across the muddy lot. The rain had morphed into a soft shower. The sky to the west was streaked with a long, low hint of light.

"We need to get out of here," she said quietly. "We need to be at the grave when she comes back. If she runs, we can follow her tracks. "We have our flashlights – right?"

Ben nodded. He didn't mention that if it kept raining, her tracks would disappear quickly. The fact that Mira wasn't considering this was a bad sign.

"Shouldn't we wait for Dad?" Ben watched his sister carefully. "He has the truck. We can cover more ground that way." He waited. "It's a little crazy, Mira, to track a coyote on foot in the rain. Don't you think?"

"No," Mira turned to face her brother. "Not if Toby comes to guide us. He called us to be here, didn't he?"

Ben didn't answer. "See if the TV works," he said, flopping back onto one of the beds. "Check for the weather channel. And keep checking your phone too.

"Keep trying – okay?" Ben rolled over. He loved his sister but this whole thing was getting to be too much. "Wake me when Dad comes," he said, pulling the pillow over his head.

CHAPTER 9

Mira waited at Toby's grave for two hours. She hoped the coyote would appear for company but since it was still raining she didn't count on it; she was really waiting for Toby.

By 8 p.m. the rain had stopped. There was a fine mist over the streetlight at the edge of town, creating a soft halo around it and laying an iridescent blanket along the road. The white chapel, alone on its little hill, glistened as Jacob approached it.

Jacob's truck stopped at the end of the curving path behind the church, idled a moment, and then was silent. He dimmed his headlights. For a moment he didn't move. He breathed deeply. Thank God she was there. Mira saw him and stood. She walked toward him slowly, her skin cold – blue like ice, but not feeling it, not even aware that she was wet.

"Mira," he called, as if to reassure her, as if she didn't know who it was.

"I'm sorry, Dad," she fell into his arms. "I'm sorry," repeating it, sobbing, at a loss to explain, at a loss to understand what she was doing there, at a loss to understand herself.

He took her back to the motel. He had gone there first, been directed to go there by Ella who was so glad to see him that she left the restaurant and personally walked him over to room #3.

"They're good kids," she had said to him, looking up as they walked, trying to see his face. "Don't be harsh with them."

"I won't," he had answered, thinking *as if I could.*

But it had been a nerve-racking day for Jacob and it showed. Worry for the children, his fears for them, plus hours of almost zero visibility as he fought his way through flooded roads and detours, had left a pall of exhaustion upon his features that silenced Ella, and that frightened Ben when the motel door opened and there his father stood, his face an ashen mask in the dull light.

"I appreciate you being here, Ben," Jacob had said, entering the room and noticing that Mira wasn't there. "It's a relief to see that you didn't let her come this far alone."

Because although that surely wasn't the reason Ben had accompanied his sister to Tobias' grave, Jacob had asked him many times to "keep an eye" on Mira, in case she got any "crazy ideas about going off somewhere."

Ben had tried to oblige but he didn't like it. The way he saw it, Mira was more intelligent and capable than he was. Jacob's request seemed sexist to Ben. "Why don't you trust her, Dad?" he had said. "Because she's a girl?"

"No, not at all," Jacob had answered. "It's because she's too much like her mother, unpredictable, might do anything – could go off someday and never come back."

So that answered it. But still, Ben didn't like it.

"I want to come with you, Dad," he had said, pulling on his jacket as they prepared to go out to the grave to look for Mira because of course that's where she would be. "Toby belonged to all of us, not just to Mira."

Jacob hadn't answered until they reached the chapel. "Toby belongs to Toby, Ben," he said, pulling into the church drive. "That's what Mira can't accept. She needs to let him go."

Ben didn't answer. How could he explain the tug on his own heart, the pounding in his own blood when the image of Tobias woke him up two nights ago? He couldn't explain Mira and he couldn't explain himself. *Sometimes a person has to be ready to understand why they do things,* he was thinking, watching Jacob walk out to Mira, watching him walk her back to the truck. *The time has to be right – no one can force it.*

"I wonder how much we should tell him," he had said to Mira, earlier that afternoon, waiting at the motel, remembering the horseback riders they had met in Tacopa.

"Probably not everything," she had answered. "At least not yet." And then she had smiled that Mira smile, the one that always reassured him that their secrets were safe. "No point letting him think we're both crazy."

They were quiet on the ride back to the motel. Ella had left some fresh rolls and a large container of hot soup by the door to room #3. "Dad," Mira asked, taking out her thermos and removing the cap to hold some soup, "you know about coyotes, right?"

Jacob nodded.

If Toby had pups last summer, wouldn't they be off on their own by now? Wouldn't the den be empty?"

"Technically, yes. But the area around it could still be home. Coyote families have many hiding places. They like to keep in touch while the pups are growing. Even when they're grown the family often travels together, especially for the first year. They have an average range of anywhere from eight to twelve miles." Jacob looked off, as if remembering some experience in the mountains.

Mira and Ben exchanged looks. How far was Tacopa? Weren't they told it was "almost twelve miles" from Shoshone?

"But it's the males that stray the farthest," Jacob was saying, "before they eventually leave for good." Jacob looked back at Mira. "The females stay with their mom."

"They do?" Mira smiled.

"Yep." Jacob smiled back at her. "They're very family oriented – like to stay close to their moms; sometimes they never leave."

"Really? They stay with her forever?"

"Well," Jacob dipped his cup into the soup for a second helping, "at least until Prince Charming comes along."

Jacob washed up and then made a space for himself along the bottom of Ben's bed, extending his legs across the room's only chair. Soon he was asleep, his gentle snoring working its magic on Ben who rolled onto his side and followed suite.

Mira sat on her bed and watched. How could they do it – go to sleep so easily, like nothing was wrong, like Toby didn't need them? How could Ben forget what they had heard in the coffee shop – hunters armed with rifles, scouring the area for pups that were very possibly Toby's and willing to kill them, to skin them for their coats. Ella had said they would be "just fine." But Ella didn't believe it. Of course not. And neither did Mira.

CHAPTER 10

The night was still and the clouds were drifting in thin wisps across the vast expanse of desert sky. High above the hills a distant moon was barely visible.

Mira slid from her bed, retrieved her dry socks from the radiator and put on her wet shoes over them. She ignored her jacket and dug out a dry shirt, a vest, and a flashlight from her backpack. Without a sound Mira crossed the room to the dresser. The keys to her father's truck glinted in the slant of light through the partially curtained window. She picked them up, opened the door and went outside. The thin flannel vest she wore over her shirt flapped in the breeze.

The truck wasn't locked. Mira climbed into the cab and slid the ignition key into place. For a moment she sat there looking out into the night. Lights were still visible in the restaurant. I wonder when they close, she was thinking. It was almost midnight.

Lost in thought, Mira was startled by the sudden appearance of a twenty year old, camouflaged pick-up with mud-caked tires that was pulling into the lot, its long-distance beams sweeping across the motel. She ducked instinctively, listening. The men – it sounded like at least four of them, were loud, cussing and laughing and whooping it up. The door to the restaurant banged closed behind them.

Mira slid to the floor and reached under the driver's seat. She felt around until she touched the cold metal of her father's gun. She pulled it out and placed it on the open floor with her flashlight where it would be easy to retrieve. *Now,* she was thinking as she backed out of the truck, *let me make sure these are the men I might have to kill.*

Mira was completely fearless and 100 percent confident when she entered the coffee shop. She ignored the noisy table of new customers, passed them and sat down at the counter a short distance away with her back to them. She asked for coffee from the cook who came out to take the new orders. He saw her, brought the coffee, and said nothing.

The conversation going on loudly at the table behind Mira was brutal. The images it evoked spread over her like heat but Mira didn't move. At all costs she needed to stay calm, remain invisible, do nothing to arouse suspicion.

Here is the conversation that she heard:

"I'll get me another one tonight, for sure," a large, round-faced man wearing camouflage is bragging to his friends, "just like the one I got a week ago." Barely pausing, he glances at the cook, "a nice juicy steak to fire me up, Sir, and a swig of whiskey to wash it down.

"Know how I got her?" Mira listens intently as the hunter lowers his voice, shifting sideways in his chair and pulling a small horn-like device from his pocket, "Lookie this, my friends."

Mira remains motionless; she doesn't turn. None of the men are aware of her.

"Listen," the camouflaged hunter leans forward and blows through the horn. The sound is chilling, like a baby's scream, like a small animal in pain. "This gets 'em every time. Stupid bitches come runnin to save their pups but what they get is a bullet in the head – POW!"

Satisfied and grinning, he leans back and blows the horn again, "Their heads just explode if you get it right – eyes pop out and everything."

That was the first bit of information that struck like a hot fist into Mira's chest.

"Didn't help you tonight, Shorty," a companion spoke from across the table. "Even with your night goggles on, didn't do you no good this time."

"The night ain't over yet, Billy-Boy. How many you caught lately?" Once again, the hunter blows the horn. "Wait and see what I got planned for that bitch behind the church."

"Now you all shut up and stop the bickering," a deeper voice cuts the air. "You're actin like a bunch of old ladies." The table becomes quiet.

The new voice has a harsh scratching quality, command-ing but dark. When it continues, there is rapt attention from the other men.

The room is still as stone. "We need to surprise that bitch behind the church – give her a real scare, make her jump off her ass and head for the hills. She's got those half-grown pups of hers hid somewhere, so while her tracks are fresh we follow. Once we find her lair we lure her out and kill her. Easy. No problem.

"Now – aha! – here comes the fun part. We scrounge around checking for those pups of hers. They're sure to be close by, two or three hiding together, scared to come out. Soon as we locate 'em, we send down one of these, throw it right at 'em – right into their hideout. "

The man who is speaking is showing something to his friends, passing it around the table. "Canister got cyanide in it," he says, "we aim it straight into their dugouts, don't matter how many of 'em in there, we trap 'em so they can't get out. Then we wait – let it work." He chuckles softly. "If we're lucky it'll kill every stinking one of them."

Mira doesn't move.

For a few moments the table is silent. The cook is bringing their food. As he passes Mira, he slides her a glance but says nothing.

"And … if a few of 'em are strong enough to climb out," the deep scratching voice continues, startling Mira, making her heart pound, " … we'll be right there to finish 'em off. We can strangle 'em one by one if we have to," he pauses for effect, "get some nice hides that way, strangle and skin 'em right on the spot, leave what's left for the birds to pick at."

A new voice enters the conversation: "These young coyotes are a good size, got nicer coats than most pups, even nicer than the bitch." The new voice sounds perfectly agreeable, actually happy about the prospect of skinning the pups!

"I seen 'em once," he continues, " – seen her runnin with them; I tried but I couldn't catch 'em. They went up between them hills on the way to Badwater, 'bout five of 'em – coats thick and pretty-like, red and gold. Can't beat that! How much you think we could fetch for one of them pelts, Billy?"

Mira got up slowly. She forgot to pay for the coffee but it didn't matter. She walked to the far end of the counter, her back still to the table of hunters. From there she pushed the swinging half door and went behind the counter and into the kitchen. She passed the cook who looked up at her and nodded slightly as she moved to the back door of the restaurant, opened it to a shock of cold air and walked towards the motel.

The cook stopped what he was doing and went to the door watching her. When she reached door #3, he returned to his work, shaking his head slowly. *The kid may be slightly off,* he was thinking, *but she's on one hell of a mission tonight.*

And she was.

CHAPTER 11

When Mira opened the door to room #3, everyone was asleep. She reclosed the door quietly, went to the truck, removed her father's gun and pushed it deep into the pocket of her vest. She took the flashlight and glanced at the keys still dangling from the ignition. Better leave them; returning them to the room wasn't worth the risk.

Mira walked with a steady pace across the lot and out onto the road leading to the chapel, the gun secure against her ribs, the flashlight straight down against her leg. The rain had stopped and the sky was black. A single distant star had appeared but the moon, still partially hidden behind the clouds, cast only a thin veil of light along the road.

Mira walked. The church when she reached it seemed to appear suddenly out of the gloom. The desert behind it lay dark and threatening with clefts of sand cut by the storm, filled with uprooted brush and other debris, making her path lumpy and hazardous. But that was fine. Mira knew exactly where she was going.

And the coyote was there.

Mira walked quietly up to the grave. An aura of calm, not

the calm before the storm but the calm that follows a storm, had enveloped her. The coyote sensing this remained motionless, ears up, watching.

Mira settled down a few feet from the grave. She glanced over at the coyote, took a long breath and let it out slowly. For several minutes she remained still, looking out into the night as the coyote watched her intently. Then she lay down and closed her eyes.

After a few moments, the coyote did the same.

When Ben awoke it was 2 a.m. He got up, rinsed off his face with just a trickle of water in order not to wake Jacob, and went outside to relieve his bladder, leaving the door ajar. He looked around. No Mira.

The night was cold. A few more stars had appeared and the moon, although still veiled, cast a faint light upon Jacob's truck. Ben walked over and looked into the empty cab hoping Mira was there, but of course she wasn't. Back in the motel room, he retrieved his jacket and was about to reach for Mira's but changed his mind.

Instead, he reached for the red shawl that lay next to her backpack. He remembered her question about the strange symbols on the shawl – what was their meaning? Ben moved to the door. Perhaps there was protection in the shawl, which was why the horseback riders had placed it over her. Ben closed the door quietly behind him. He hoped so.

As soon as he recognized Mira, Ben hastened his pace, crossing to Toby's grave with long steps, walking as fast as was practical among the mounds of wet sand, the zigzag of storm forged channels appearing unexpectedly along the desert floor.

At first he thought he saw the dark form of the coyote lying next to her, but getting closer he realized she was alone. He stopped. "Mira?"

Mira sat up. "Ben," she reached for her flashlight but stopped, looking over to where the coyote had been resting. "You sacred her off," she whispered. "She was there – right there," Mira motioned to the stone where the coyote had lain.

"Sorry." Ben bent forward, peering at his sister, "Are you okay?"

Mira nodded.

"Here, use this," he tossed the shawl. "It's cold."

Mira caught the shawl and wrapped it around her shoulders.

"What's that?" Ben pointed to a bulge on the ground beside his sister.

"My flashlight," Mira lifted the flashlight for Ben to see. She leaned back slightly, hoping he hadn't noticed the gun that was partially hidden behind her.

But he had seen it, all right.

"Want me to wait with you?" Ben moved to clear a place to sit beside her. He looked off to the hills behind them. "She'll come back, Mira."

"No, she won't," Mira spoke with authority, the "big sister" kind of authority, "not if there's two of us. You should go, Ben. Really. Go. Come back when it's light."

"You sure?" Ben hesitated.

Mira nodded. "When Dad wakes up tell him you saw me

and I'm okay. Tell him I need to be alone." She paused, "Will you do it?"

Ben sighed, "Okay, you're the boss." He turned to go but then turned back. "I'll bring you some coffee when the restaurant opens."

Mira smiled. "Thanks a lot," she whispered. And again, as he was leaving, "Thanks, Ben."

Sound carries in the open desert. Gunshots are sharp, hard and crisp. Even from a distance, they sear through space, cutting the air and vibrating like pulses of light against the human ear. They penetrate skin, eyelids, dreams.

"My God!" Jacob sat up. He looked across towards Mira's bed, "Ben, where is she?"

"At the grave," Ben was already up, moving towards the door. "Let's go."

"Where are my keys?" Jacob swept the top of the dresser, trying not to panic, "Ben, where are they? My keys – where are they?"

Ben opened the door. "I don't know." He switched on the light and was scanning the room. "Maybe you left them in the truck."

Jacob walked outside. "I'll check. They've got to be somewhere.

"Looks like you were right," Jacob said moments later, as Ben climbed into the truck beside him. "Must have left them in the ignition; getting absent–minded in my old age."

But Jacob knew exactly where he had left the keys. And he knew who had considered taking his truck but thank God had changed her mind. *She's all right,* he told himself, *just impulsive. She'll be all right.* And he swung the truck towards the road.

CHAPTER 12

Coyotes are fast – like bullets, so fast they are visible at 04:00:00:00, and invisible at 04:00:00:01. We're talking milliseconds. Zip! Gone.

Humans just aren't that fast. So when Mira woke to the single gunshot, Toby's gravestone was already empty. She scrambled to her feet and looked around. The hunters could be heard but all was darkness at the end of the drive behind the chapel. Not until their truck started up and the lights came on would she fully realize what had happened. She crouched. Had they seen her too?

She listened. They were arguing.

"What'd you do that for, you stupid ijot?"

"I got her. I think I got her. Let's go see if I got her."

"For what? You got nothing, Shorty. She's gone."

"I think there was two of 'em. I'm goin out there, Billy. I need to go out there."

"You need to get back in the truck and shut-up.

"Look," the voice that was Billy's lowered but was still clear. "We're wasting time. Let's go. We can take the hill trail, snake around that first rock and hide the truck. Got it?"

"Good idea," another voice. "She'll be back. She always comes back. Who's got the beer?"

Mira could hear the scuffling of feet. She held her breath.

One of the truck doors slammed shot. "Okay. Ready? Somebody sit on Shorty; he's in the back with the beer. Let's go."

Motor starting; fog lights on.

Mira waited, watching the truck circle north and creep up what must have been a passable trail before the storm. The dark form of the truck bounced along like a giant groundhog, then disappeared behind a low hill.

Time to go. *Help me find her, Toby*, she prayed, *I can't do this without you.*

By the time Ben and Jacob arrived at the church, rounding the narrow drive behind it and bumping along into the desert toward Tobias' grave, Mira was gone and the hunters were gone. Well, actually, the hunters were still hunkered down in their hiding place halfway up the rocky hill.

The desert was deeply shaded, shrouded in silence. Ben and Jacob left the truck and began to walk. All that remained by the grave was the red blanket – Mira's shawl. Her footprints leading back into the hills were soon lost. Jacob's flashlight was useless; the night seemed darker, more ominous than ever. They stopped walking.

"There's too much debris out here – can't see where we're going."

"I know. It's not worth it. We need headlights. Let's go back for the truck."

Good, Ben was thinking. The truck would give some protection too.

They had almost arrived back at the truck when half-way up a long hill to the north, the hunters' truck crept out from behind its hiding place, and began creeping further up the trail, fog lights on.

"There's a road up there," Jacob watched as the truck rocked to a stop. "We should try it. If we get up high enough we can signal Mira. When the sky lightens maybe we'll see her. We'll know where to go.

"Maybe … " Jacob's voice changed suddenly, "maybe whoever is behind those lights knows exactly where she is. Maybe …" Jacob began to continue but Ben stopped him.

"They're just hunters, Dad. Who else would be out here?"

But Ben's heart was pounding too. They had reached their truck and Jacob, his head down and in no mood for conversation, was climbing in. Ben climbed in beside him.

"I bet she's close by," Ben looked over at his father, "burrowed in with the coyote, hiding from that same truck."

Jacob paused, his hand on the ignition. "What coyote?"

"The one at Toby's grave. Mira made friends with her." He stopped, not wanting to explain.

Jacob started the motor, "What? What are you saying, Ben? That's insane, hiding with a coyote. It's crazy!"

"No it's not." The truck began to move towards the trail, lunging forward as the climbing gear engaged. "Not if they're being shot at. What do you expect them to do?"

Ben paused. "Mira can take care of herself, Dad," he continued in a slow, serious tone. "Those hunters better hope they *don't* find her."

For a moment Ben waited, not sure of how much he should say; then he just went ahead and took the plunge, "She's got…"

"Got what?" Jacob was staring straight ahead, his face set. "Mira's got what?"

"Your gun – she's got your gun."

Jacob leaned down and felt under the seat. "Good God," he straightened. "Never mind, hold on. We're going to catch whoever is on that hill. They must know something."

When Jacob's truck, still on the trail, arrived as close as possible to the hunters' partially camouflaged vehicle which was, at that point, trying to secure another hiding place by backing up behind some brush closer to the top of the hill, Billy was in their headlights, his rifle pointing straight at them. They stopped.

"Who the hell are you?" Billy asked, coming up to Jacob's window.

"Have you seen anyone walking? I'm looking for my daughter. She was down there by the church."

"No. Ain't seen her. Ain't seen no one. You best get off this trail. It ain't safe up here.

"Hey!" he called to Ben. "Where you think you're goin?" Because Ben was headed over to the hunters' vehicle.

"Leave him be," Jacob was out of the truck. "He's check-ing to make sure his sister's not over there."

Billy blocked Jacob's path. "Look here, I could end this right now and bury you both so you'd never be found. If you have a badge you'd better show it cuz your story about a girl is as lame as they come. We're hunters. We got some beer in the truck, some ammo, that's all."

"She's not there," Ben was on the way back.

"Did you look in the back? How many men in the cab?"

"Four. This one makes five. Nothing in the back but gear. It's okay, Dad."

Jacob backed up. His tone changed, "Let us pass. We need to follow the trail up farther."

Billy stepped aside, "There's nothing up there. Trail's washed out. Nothin down the other side neither, nothing but wasteland and wild dogs, packs of 'em – run with the native kids.

"Ain't safe." Billy had lowered his gun. "You need to go back where you come from fore you get hurt."

"That's our decision. Now move aside," Jacob opened the door to his truck. "We're going up far as we can."

Billy nodded, moving off the trail.

"Them two are crazy as they come," he said to one of the other hunters who approached him watching Jacob pull away. "Must be the moon," he added, looking up at the pale orb, barely visible in the clouded sky, "brings out the loony tunes."

A third hunter had ambled over, his voice gravely with sleep, "Some folks just born stupid." He looked at Billy, "Am I right?"

"Yep," Billy nodded in agreement. "Game is sparse enough over there. Strangers like them two try runnin it down, they'll get a few arrows in their butts. Maybe buck-shot," and Billy chuckled at the thought.

The hunters arrived back at their truck in silence. Billy began to open the driver's side door but stopped. Suddenly he laughed. "Lookin for some girl. Ha! Sure they are." And then he laughed again. "As if we're fools."

CHAPTER 13

Whatever inspired Billy & company to leave their hideout shortly after Ben and Jacob disappeared is a mystery. Out of beer, it's a good guess they were getting edgy. Never mind if it made sense or not, five grown men (Shorty had sobered up) crammed together for thirty minutes in a short-bed pickup can't be expected to reason things out.

Using night goggles, they had emerged from the truck occasionally to check for the coyote but she had not come back and was probably gone for the night.

So, following their own advice, they backed down the trail to the desert floor and began bumping along in their mud splattered pick-up, stopping, getting out with flashlights to look for tracks, getting in again, so on and so forth.

Fate is strange. Due to the damp ground and an amazing piece of luck, they were actually able to locate the female's tracks and confirm the direction in which she was headed.

Soon however, the tracks were lost. Nevertheless, they plodded on blindly, rounding the low hills and climbing onto the hood of the truck with binoculars, as the first rocky clusters of emerging mountains appeared like ghosts in the distance.

When the sky to the east showed just a hint of grey, they left the truck. Confident that the day's first light would soon appear, they began walking towards the distant rocks in a line. Only Billy, who wasn't sure he liked the way this episode was going, stayed behind to watch the truck.

The men, no longer bogged down by the prospect of more failure, began to walk with new energy. A thermos of lukewarm coffee was passed around. The air was clear. With silent deliberation they focused on the mountain base ahead. Their vision sharpened; now they could see outlines. Soon the individual rocks that climbed into the dark hills would be visible.

Five minutes … ten minutes….

They kept walking but more slowly. No one spoke. The female's hidden lair could not be far. She would be hiding among the large stone outcrops that rose before them. There was plenty of thick brush between the stones, good prospects for dens.

The men kept pace with one another, slow and steady, scanning the rocks until they narrowed in on what seemed the ideal place to conceal a den. Yes, that would be where she would hide her pups, deep in the brush that was fast becoming visible in the semi-darkness.

And then the men were sure of it. They could sense her. She was less than 80 yards away on the hill before them.

The men slowed. They strained to see any movement, any hint of her presence. She would be watching them, her breath on the branches, the leaves … five more yards … ten …

…

Wait! … a glint of gold … there … another! Yes! And there she was! Jackpot!

"I see her. Woo-hoo! We got her!"

Mira saw her too, at almost the same instant but from higher up on the rocky hill. She had followed the coyote by pure instinct, climbing for hours between the clusters of rock and boulder until she had stopped for breath just as the sky began to lighten. From where she stood now she could see a long narrow canyon at the foot of the hill.

She angled carefully down the steep grade toward the base of the mountain but stopped half way, not wanting to risk sliding into the gorge. Beneath her, the coyote was lying in a dense thicket of undergrowth next to what looked like an opening in the brush, her tan coat a soft russet in the pale light. Why was she not burrowed in with her pups, Mira wondered.

Mira crouched down. She could make out the hunters' truck in the distance. Four of the men were approaching with what seemed to be extreme caution. A fifth man could be seen on the truck's hood, possibly with a rifle – she couldn't tell.

But none of that mattered. The hunters would soon discover they were blocked. As close as they might come to the hill from which she watched, the steep sliding walls of the narrow canyon below her would stop them.

Mira scrambled behind a rock to be sure she could not be seen. The hunters had paused. Two of them moved closer to the shadowed fissure at the base of the hill and began to check it out. After a few minutes, the other men joined them and all four began walking north, skirting the canyon's edge, looking for a way to cross.

The coyote watched. Mira watched. The men disappeared. The sky lightened.

Mira had just decided she would slide down to join the coyote when the first cry rang out. It came from the direction of the distant truck. Mira crept from behind the rock and shielded her eyes from the emerging light. Someone lay on the ground beside the truck.

Another cry of pain, this time closer. Mira stood, straining to see beyond the rocky outcrop which had blocked her view to the north. One of the four who had been walking along the far side of the gorge, was down. Slowly he got up and resumed walking. Mira searched the hills around her – empty. The desert stretching east and north. Empty.

So absorbed was Mira in the spectacle playing out before her, she never noticed that the coyote was gone. When she did notice, she made her way carefully down to the suspected den. Were the pups in there? They must be, she reasoned, which meant their mother would soon be back.

Mira sat down. The desert was quiet. She wondered if the men had given up or if they were still traveling parallel to the sharp cleft at the base of the hill, searching for a way to cross it. She laid the gun on her lap and waited.

For almost twenty minutes, Mira stayed guard at the mouth of the silent den.

Where was everyone? She stood and climbed a few yards up the hill until she could see where the truck had been. It was gone. As she moved to return to the den her attention caught on some objects scattered on the far side of the canyon to the north where one of the men had fallen. What were they? Bird feathers? Had the hunters shot some birds? But there had been no gunshots.

Mira sat down. She was puzzled. Why had the coyote abandoned her lair? Had the hunters seen her? Was she leading them off deep into the hills? Well, the coyote needn't worry. She, Mira, would stay right here and protect the pups.

Mira was exhausted. She lay down, curled onto her side, and closed her eyes. The sun was still hiding behind the mountains to her east and the wind was cold. She remembered the shawl – where had she dropped it? Slowly the wind died down.

Her sleep deepened. Where were Ben and her father? And what about the three on horseback? They had been to Toby's grave but where were they now?

And then he came.

This time she was sure that he was real, not a dream, not an angel – well, maybe an angel. She even recognized his horse, Molly. He was smiling when he woke her. He told her to come with him, that the den was empty. "Come on," he said, reaching down to swing her up behind him, amazing her with his strength, making her wonder if a human could be that strong.

But of course she loved it. The ride was incredible, holding on tight, her arms around him, laying her face against his back, his long hair flying over her. It was a magical ride, one she would never forget. Mile after mile they rode in the glow of an emerging dawn.

Finally, as Molly climbed and turned, as the mare slowed and carefully descended between the rocks, then stretched out her long legs and loped gently on more steady ground, Mira closed her eyes. She was safe. Everything would be all right.

He stopped several yards before reaching Toby's grave. "Here?" he asked her, turning slightly so that she glimpsed his eyes.

Mira shook herself awake, "Yes, this is perfect."

Mira slid down from Molly and looked up at the young man with a question in her eyes.

"Kwinaa," he said in answer. "It means the Eagle, I have the blessings of the Eagle." He moved Molly closer to the grave, studying the stone. Mira walked with them.

"I'm Mira, maybe you remember ..." she stopped, blushing. He didn't answer. Instead he smiled at her, a smile that melted her heart completely. Of course he remembered.

Kwinaa, she spoke his name without a sound. The eagle. Kwinn.

Mira stood silent as she watched him go. There wasn't a whole lot she could count on these days, but she knew one thing for certain: she could count on Kwinn.

Mira looked back sadly at Tobias' lonely grave. She saw the blanket on the ground where she had dropped it, reached for it and put it around her shoulders like a shawl.

The air was still, no wind, no breeze – the mystical hush between dawn and day. Lost in thought, Mira knelt and slowly traced Tobias' name on the stone – once, then once again. And then she looked up. And the coyote was there.

Mira caught her breath. Was it just the light? The female looked so perfect, so beautiful. And then, standing a little distance away, she saw the pup – a half-grown image of Tobias, same silky bronze coat, same long waving tail. But otherwise the pup, long legged and thin was the image of his mother, or rather of *her* mother.

She has amber eyes, Mira was thinking, *golden jewels just like her mom's.*

Thank you, Toby, she prayed, her hand still on the stone over his grave, for letting me see her, for letting me know that she lives – like you.

Tobias Lives, she was thinking. *That's what should be on the gravestone*: *Tobias Lives.*

But it wasn't over yet. Not by a long shot.

CHAPTER 14

Say what you will but hunters, whether you appreciate them or not, can be very good at what they do. They can track through hills of rock, through mounds of branch and brush and gravel. They can isolate the marks of one amid dozens, sense movement where no movement is seen. They can distinguish fear in their prey; they can distinguish exhaustion.

Hunters care nothing for time. They can pursue for hours, days, weeks, holding perfect silence, keeping perfect focus as they mark and follow, creep and crawl, close in upon and finish off their prey.

Usually. Usually they can do this. Unless the hunters are human, weakened, injured, and dealing with pain.

But even then, with the pain still fresh from an unknown source, the burn of an arrow deep in his flesh, even then an experienced hunter can ignore it all, can use the pain to fuel new strength, new urgency to finish the chase whatever it takes.

It was almost full light as Mira sat peacefully by the grave. No hunters in sight. If they had not yet abandoned the chase, Mira guessed that soon, with the heat of day upon them, they would be forced to give it up.

But Mira was wrong. The men had no intention of giving up. Moving along the gorge for at least a mile, they had focused for some sign of the coyote only to realize that she had outsmarted them again. But this time it was different. This time they knew where she had gone. This time they knew exactly where to find her.

And so they had reversed. They weren't worried at all. Success, however long it took, was all that mattered. And so, they turned around without complaint, got into their truck and backtracked along their trail of the previous night.

Until they sensed that they were close enough. They slowed. This was it.

The truck stopped and the sun was full. No one spoke as the truck was silenced and the men emerged and walked slowly across the desert floor. Only the sound of their boots, their footsteps, could be heard. 100 yards. 200 yards. The walk of death.

Even before the grave was in sight, even before they could see Tobias' mate, her rich, soft coat the prize they were seeking, they knew she was there. They knew without words that her end was near. And it was.

The hunter responsible for the final kill will take his time. He will move with stealth upon sighting his prey; he will pause and crouch, listen and breathe softly. Then, with the end no longer in doubt, he will stop all movement. He will wait, still as stone. His soul will merge with the soul of his prey; he will ask for her life.

Then ... slowly ... when the moment is right, he will rise up unseen – like a snake ... and strike!

Swift and sure Death comes to his prey. One bullet. Down. Eyes clouding over. Finished.

And so it was for the coyote that had loved Tobias.

Once the shot had been fired, the hunters, as if on cue, began to walk, slowly at first, … five paces … ten … closing in upon their prize with measured steps. Now they stopped, standing upright, weapons lowered.

"There's another, a young one – see him? He ain't runnin. Looks frozen."

"Lemme get him, Billy."

"Wait." Billy extended his arm, blocking the other hunter. "What the hell … ??"

Mira, who had been unnoticed until this moment, sitting motionless a few feet from the grave with her shawl draped over her arms and back, had felt the shot, felt it slam into the coyote. At first it had numbed her, a bolt to her senses.

And then she saw it … the body down … sinking … draining …

Mira fumbled for her father's gun. "No … NO!" She struggled to her feet, her father's handgun held high, aimed in the direction from which the shot was fired. Slowly she lowered it.

The hunters were visible to her now, each one distinct. She moved the gun slowly aligning it evenly with the man in the center of the group. "DON'T MOVE!"

But no one was moving; they were just standing there staring at her.

Mira walked to the body and crouched beside it, and then without warning a wall of grief moved over her, pushing her down, weakening her. She closed her own eyes and reached to close the eyes of the dead animal. She tried to stand but couldn't, bending and supporting herself with her hands on her knees. She looked down at the closed eyes. Golden eye-lashes. *Oh, God, it can't be true. Don't let it be true!*

The men were talking: "Someone's doing somethin over there. I don't like it. Gonna say they got there first. Not gonna let us get our pelts." They waited.

Mira was placing her shawl over the body of the female when she looked up and saw the pup, saw the terror in the young one's eyes. "Go," she was sobbing. "Run!" But the frightened pup wouldn't go; instead she moved closer to Mira.

"Okay ... okay ... don't be afraid." Mira was standing now, tears blinding her but no longer sobbing, arms out-stretched, waving the gun at the small group of hunters who had begun moving again ... slowly approaching the grave, slowly approaching the terrified pup.

"STAY AWAY FROM HER. GO AWAY!" She was yell-ing now – not screaming, yelling a wild, frightening kind of yell from deep in her throat, a yell that hung in the air, reso-nated, meant absolute business. "THAT'S MY DOG. YOU KILL MY DOG AND I'LL KILL YOU. YOU KILL HER AND I'LL KILL YOU ALL." She began walking towards the men, squinting at them to clear her vision, aiming the gun from one end of the line to the other.

Billy backed up a step and turned to the other men. "Girl is crazy," he said quietly. "Got a gun. Looks crazy enough to use it."

"Where'd she come from? Who is she, Billy? Maybe we should call her bluff."

Billy studied Mira; he glanced at the shawl she had be-gun to lay carefully over the dead coyote, it's pattern and origin clear.

"Not worth the risk." Billy scanned the surrounding desert. "Move on her now and we start a war." He looked at the other men. "Not worth it," he repeated.

"Let's go," he said with finality. "Leave the girl out of it."

And so they turned. And walked away.

CHAPTER 15

Not until Jacob and Ben reached the bottom of the trail, did they hear the shot that killed Tobias' mate. A few moments later, just as they reached the drive behind the chapel the hunters' truck appeared. In a churn of dust and sand, it lurched onto the road and roared past them.

Ben and Jacob continued to the end of the drive and stopped.

"There she is," Ben spoke. "See her? She's okay."

Jacob nodded. For a few minutes they sat together in the truck, not speaking, watching Mira. Neither made an attempt to move, to interrupt the scene that was unfolding before them.

Mira knelt by the dead female. Gently she lifted the shawl and stroked the damp fur. "It's all right," she whispered, "It's over now." She looked up. The young female was standing a few feet away, watching. She took a step towards the body of her mother, wide-eyed and terror-struck.

Mira replaced the shawl around the female's bleeding neck, leaving only her thin legs and perfectly formed head, showing only the closed eyes, the soft ears, the narrow jaw and the mouth that would never open again, never sing, never smile. "I'm sorry . . . I'm so sorry," she whispered. "I let Tobias down. I let you down."

Mira sank back on her heels. She looked at the lanky copy of a young Tobias and thought her heart would break. "You're very beautiful," she said softly. "You look just like your daddy ... well, almost like your daddy, but also like your beautiful mother."

The female pup was still. Suddenly she looked towards the distant hill. "Are your brothers up there?" Mira followed her gaze but could see nothing. "They're almost grown by now, aren't they? But what about you?" The young coyote looked back at Mira. "You don't have anyone, do you?" Mira continued quietly. "You're all alone."

Mira paused. "But ... you can have me. At least, I'm someone."

Mira wiped her eyes with her hand. The young coyote was still looking at her. "Do you want to come home with me?" Mira tried to smile. She opened her hand and held it out to the pup. The coyote took another step towards her.

Mira's hand was trembling. "We're moving to a new place in the mountains and we need protection up there." She was speaking now in a matter of fact tone, a conversational tone.

The pup relaxed, listening intently.

"And ... " Mira stood up slowly, "if you come with me ... " she started walking, all the while aware of the long legs and nervous gait of the young coyote following, "you can be free to go anytime. It's up to you. I promise."

The coyote moved a few steps closer and then began

to travel side by side with her. "Because, you know," Mira spoke in a confidential tone as she neared her father and Ben, "after awhile your Prince Charming may come along."

"This is my new friend, she told her father. Okay?"

Jacob smiled. He nodded, his eyes filling. "Mira, we need to bury her mother. We need to bury her beside Tobias." He paused. "Stay here. I'll do it."

Mira stood silently with the coyote beside her as the air warmed and her father walked to the grave, a long shovel from the back of his truck swinging beside him. His steps seemed slow. *My dad is getting old,* she thought. *Forty-four is pretty old.*

"We better be careful to take good care of him," she said to the coyote, sitting down and reaching out to touch her. The coyote shivered a little under her touch. But it was just a ripple. She never moved from her place by Mira.

When Ben came over and sat down beside them, they were peaceful and still – all three.

"What happened to you?" Mira asked.

"Truck overturned, slid down a gully. We tried everything to get it out. Lucky for us some horseback riders came along, pulled it out no problem." Ben paused. And then he looked at Mira with that look that meant they were still just as much co-conspirators as ever.

"There were three of them," he said. "One was a young girl." And he smiled. "She said to say hi."

FINIS

Following is an excerpt from
Tobias book 3

THE SONS OF TOBIAS

CHAPTER 1

B andit saw his sister go. He was almost half a mile
away on one of the low hills west of his father's grave.
They all had heard the gunshot – all four brothers coming to a sudden halt wherever they were, braking to
a standstill in the cool air, their ears pointed, heads turning
slowly towards the deathly stillness that followed the crack
of the bullet's release.

For a moment none had moved – still as statues of bronze,
their reddish coats soft, glistening from winter, their golden
eyes like jewels, each one alert, each one knowing without
knowing as the bullet struck, aware without allowing the
awareness to be full, to render them helpless. Then bolting
suddenly, frightened, dissolving into the brown hills, the desert slopes, obeying the lesson their mother had taught them to
run, to hide, to disappear as coyotes can do so well, melting
into air, fading into earth and brush, hearts pounding, blood
rushing – gone.

Until there was only one who stood his ground, who did
not run. Bandit, moving as in a dream slowly toward the
sound of the gunshot, not away from it, moving toward the

grave of his father where night after night his mother had lain keeping watch for Tobias, waiting for the miracle that was not to be, guarding the silent crumbling body while she sang for his spirit to return.

Bandit, knowing … knowing where the bullet had struck … moving … moving. And then he stopped, frozen as rock, up on the ridge above the desert floor as the minutes passed and one by one his brothers emerged, padding softly up behind him, standing together under the vast ivory sky of dawn, watching the scene unfold below.

He saw his sister. She was there, standing close to a young girl who was down on the ground trying but unable to stand, forced to her knees again and again, crawling slowly while his sister watched, crawling to his mother who lay in her blood on his father's grave.

The girl's thin arm was up and she was waving something small – a weapon, at a band of men who were watching her. They were taking hesitant steps toward her, towards his sister who stood trembling beside her, men with rifles, shotguns, seeing his sister's terror, hoping to approach her while the death terror held her frozen – her body numbed, eyes locked, white as ice. What did they want from her? To kill her too? To rip her coat from her? To steal her thick and beautiful coat?

But then they stopped walking. They were fearful of the girl, of her weapon. She stood slowly, facing them, waving the weapon. And a terrible cry of grief went out from her, and the men backed up and turned away, acknowledging the power of that cry, unable to confront it.

Bandit studied the girl. Her hair was long and dark and

she wore the shawl of the Shoshone. *Friend*, thought Bandit. *Shoshone are friends, protect my mother, protect my sister. Shoshone stand proud against evil men.*

Bandit took a few steps away from the rocks. He turned to catch the attention of his brothers. The men who sent death to their mother must not be feared; they must be punished. But this would be another day.

Now, he told them, eyes closed, bones rigid as he stood tall before them, now was a time for silence, for calm, for an affirmation that although their mother's life was ending in this world, she would be able to bless them from the next.

So the brothers stood close to one another, their shoulders touching. In this way they drew strength from each other. They could wait for their revenge. They knew that theirs was a power that would prevail even as it had prevailed for thousands of years. And the desert blessed these brothers of the empty land, the endless sky. And peace entered into them.

The four brothers were seven months old; they had left the den long ago, traveling at first with their mother and their sister, hunting and playing as a family, venturing off on their own only for a day or two but always returning to their mother's lair, proud to protect her, proud to protect their only sister. She was smaller and thinner than her brothers, shy and gentle, a shadow of her mother with the same golden eyes that their father, long-haired renegade canine protector, had loved so much, so desperately.

Bandit remained by his rock as one by one his brothers moved away. He watched the girl for a long time after the shot that had entered his mother and caused the slow expanding pool of blood beneath her. He studied the protective movements of the girl as she placed her shawl over the still body and reached out to comfort the slight trembling form of his sister.

The men had left, turning, retreating to their truck, kicking up dirt and sand as they sped off to the east. But then, down by the little chapel close to the road, another truck appeared and stopped, and after a few moments the girl began walking toward it.

Bandit watched his sister follow the girl, a few paces behind, wobbling on her long legs, closer and closer to the truck by the road.

A man from the truck went to the girl and embraced her. He walked out to the grave then, carrying a long shovel and Bandit understood what would be done.

The man buried Bandit's mother with reverence, leaving the protective shawl upon her, which was right and good. Until it was finished and the man walked back to the road, and Bandit knew sorrow for the first time in his life as he looked at the empty ground and the sad mound of earth beneath which his mother lay.

He thought of his sister then. Where would she go? She had clung to her mother, seeming too fragile to run with her brothers, unable to keep up with their bursts of speed, their twists and turns, the roughness with which they tested each other's strength. But all that must change now. They would teach her, encourage her, until she grew to be one of them.

Bandit sighed. He looked out toward the road. And then he looked again. She was gone. She had vanished. And the truck also was gone.

To be continued

BOOKS BY BOBBI BOLAND WHITE

ESCAPE FROM MARIANNA, available in print and digital. Young Adult award-winner, 2011. Kirkus review.

TOBIAS TRILOGY:
Recommended: Teen through Adult

A PRAYER FOR TOBIAS, Available in print and digital, mid 2017.

TOBIAS RETURNS: *A CALL FOR HELP.* Available in print and digital, fall, 2017.

THE SONS OF TOBIAS, Available in print and digital, fall, 2017.

Author information: Bobbi Boland White, author

AMAZON: Bobbi Boland White: books

TWITTER: Bobbi.White,BBWhite @bbwmanagement

(https//twitter.com/bbwmanagement Message me!
bbwmanagement@aol.com
Bobbi.white1@aol.com

www.ingramcontent.com/pod-product-compliance
Lightning Source LLC
Chambersburg PA
CBHW030539180626
46810CB00005B/1930